D0250053

This book is a work of fiction. Any references to historical events, real people, or real places are used fictitiously. Other names, characters, places, and events are products of the author's imagination, and any resemblance to actual events or places or persons, living or dead, is entirely coincidental.

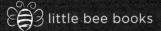 little bee books

An imprint of Bonnier Publishing USA
251 Park Avenue South, New York, NY 10010
Copyright © 2019 by Bonnier Publishing USA
All rights reserved, including the right of reproduction in whole or in part in any form.
Little Bee Books is a trademark of Bonnier Publishing USA, and associated colophon is a trademark of Bonnier Publishing USA.
Library of Congress Cataloging-in-Publication Data
is available upon request.
Printed in China TPL 0119
ISBN 978-1-4998-0806-3 (hardcover)
First Edition 10 9 8 7 6 5 4 3 2 1
ISBN 978-1-4998-0805-6 (paperback)
First Edition 10 9 8 7 6 5 4 3 2 1
ISBN 978-1-4998-0807-0 (ebook)

littlebeebooks.com
bonnierpublishingusa.com

Newton, A. I., author.
Up, up, and away!

2019
33305244116624
gi   03/15/19

W

ALIEN NEXT DOOR

UP, UP, AND AWAY!

by A. I. Newton

illustrated by Anjan Sarkar

little bee books

TABLE OF CONTENTS

HOME, AT LAST

HARRIS WALKER AND HIS FRIEND Zeke were walking home from school. They were both in great moods.

"Spring Break!" Harris shouted. "A whole week off from school! We can hang out and do whatever we want!"

"And this happens the same time every year?" asked Zeke.

"Pretty much," replied Harris.

"Hmm . . ." said Zeke. "Back home on Tragas, breaks only happen after we learn how to do something really well. Then we spend the whole break in meditation pods reviewing all we've learned up to that point."

Harris smiled. Zeke had very quickly become one of his best friends. He still found it amazing that Zeke was from another planet.

"That sounds okay, I guess. Since you're probably learning how to move things with your mind!" Harris said. "But is it as much fun as the time we went camping?"

"I have to admit, I didn't understand at first why anyone would want to sleep outside," Zeke said. "But once we did it, I did have fun."

"And I'll never forget the look on your face when you first saw a waterfall here," Harris said.

Zeke smiled. "I could not believe that the water flowed down from the top," he said. "On Tragas, waterfalls flow up!"

"I'd love to see that!" said Harris.

"You never know," said Zeke. "Maybe some day, you'll get to visit Tragas."

"I don't know if I could survive eating only Tragas food," said Harris. "Remember the first time my parents saw food from your planet?"

"I sure do," said Zeke. "They were polite to my parents, but I could see that they were a little freaked out."

"I was, too!" said Harris. "When I saw those slimy purple slugs your folks brought . . ."

"Kreslars," Zeke said. "They are the most popular food on Tragas."

"Yeah, well, I wouldn't open a Kreslar stand on Earth," Harris joked. "I don't think you'd sell very many."

Zeke laughed. "I guess, but there are a lot of things about Earth that I still don't completely get. Like Halloween and Valentine's Day. They both turned out to be fun, but I still think they are kind of weird."

The boys arrived at their houses, which were next door to each other.

"Come over and hang out after dinner?" Harris asked as he opened the front door to his house.

"Sure," said Zeke. "See you later."

As he walked across his front lawn, Zeke thought about how, after a hard beginning, he really was enjoying his time here on Earth now. Then he walked through his front door.

Zeke was shocked to see his parents packing things into boxes.

"What's going on?" he asked.

"Guess what, Zeke?" said Xad, his father. "We're going home . . . to Tragas!"

ZEKE WAS BEYOND STUNNED.
He stared at his parents, speechless.

He always knew that some day he'd
have to leave Earth, just like he had
left every other place he'd lived. After
all, his parents were researchers. Their
job was to move from planet to planet,
studying each world's habits, customs,
and culture.

But Zeke had never been given so much as a hint that his parents were close to wrapping up their time on Earth.

"What is all this about?" he asked. "I mean, why now? Why is it time to leave?"

"Xad and I have collected all the research we were sent here for. So we need to go back to Tragas to get our next assignment," explained Quar, his mother.

Zeke's shoulders slumped and his chin dropped to his chest. *Here I go again*, he thought. *Another new planet, another new school, new kids, new games, holidays, customs. New everything . . . again!* Zeke was tired of doing this over and over.

He suddenly realized that of all the worlds he'd lived on, Earth had become his favorite. And now this!

Zeke tried to compose himself.

"So your research on Earth is done?" he asked.

"Correct," replied Xad. "We have learned a lot, though."

"Yes, we learned that humans require many different types of clothing," Quar said. "They need clothing for warm weather, cold weather, wet weather, windy weather. Very different from Tragas. As you know, Zeke, all our clothing looks the same."

"Yes, and our clothing adjusts for the weather conditions, so we never have to change it," Xad added.

"We also learned that humans like to cook their food many different ways—using stoves, ovens, microwaves, grills, and open fires," said Quar. "All we do to cook food is release a small amount of pulsar rays from our fingers."

Quar's fingertips started glowing bright red.

"Oh, and don't forget," Xad said. "We now know that humans grow most of their food in plastic containers and glass jars. They pick them right off long, flat trees called 'shelves' that grow inside giant markets."

"So you see, there is not much left for us to learn," Quar said.

"Sure there is," said Zeke, hoping to convince his parents to stay on Earth a little longer. "There's holidays, and camping, and baseball, and soccer, and—"

"Well," Xad interrupted. "It sounds like you've been doing some research of your own, Zeke. I'm very proud of you. Maybe you'll grow up to be a researcher, too."

"But, I—"

"Zeke, you can fill us in on all you've learned on the trip back to Tragas," Xad interrupted again. "But now, we have to finish packing."

Zeke sighed.

"You seem upset by this news, Zekelabraxis," said Quar, using Zeke's full Tragas name. "On every planet we've lived, you've always been in a hurry to get back to Tragas. We thought you'd be happy to go home."

"Well, Earth is different," Zeke said. "I've made some good friends here, like Roxy and Harris."

Harris! he thought. *How am I going to tell Harris?!*

QUAR GAVE ZEKE A HUG. "Don't you want to see Tragas again?" she asked.

"Sure, someday," he replied. "But right now, I'm settled here. I know things were a little tough for me at the start, but I'm happy now. I don't want to go back yet."

Zeke placed his fingertips against his forehead. Using his mind projection powers, he made the tops of the boxes his parents had been packing fly open. Out flew lamps, books, clothing, cups, and plates.

"Zeke, please don't unpack these boxes," said Xad. "Your mother and I have worked very hard to load them carefully. I'm sorry, but we really need to go home to Tragas."

Zeke's hands dropped to his sides. A stack of books that had been floating in the air crashed to the floor. A kitchen bowl landed on the couch.

Zeke turned and ran out the front door. He was so upset, he could hardly think straight. His mind raced with thoughts of leaving Earth, his friends, and this world he had come to know.

Then he turned and hurried next door to Harris's house. Zeke knocked on the front door.

I have to talk to Harris, he thought.

"Hi, Zeke," said Harris's dad. "Come on in. Harris is upstairs."

"Thanks, Mr. Walker," Zeke said, trying not to show how upset he was. He bounded up the stairs and found Harris in his room.

"Dude, check this out," Harris said, picking up a comic book. "It's the latest issue of *Tales from Alien Worlds*! In this story, a tiny spaceship lands on the roof of a house. But it's so small that nobody—"

"Harris!" Zeke interrupted him.

"Whoa, what's wrong? You look really sad," said Harris.

"My parents are taking me back to Tragas!"

Harris was stunned.

"What?! I . . . I . . . " he stammered, trying to find the right words. "I mean . . . I feel like we just met, but you've already become one of my best friends. I can't believe you have to leave now. Why?"

"My parents said that they finished their research here on Earth," Zeke explained. "So, it's time to go home."

"But this planet *is* your home now," Harris said.

"Yes, it feels that way to me, too," said Zeke. "I have been through this so many times, and I still never get used to it. But this time is by far the worst. I've never made friends like you and Roxy anywhere else. And now I have to go."

"No," Harris said. "I won't let you just leave that easily."

"But what are we going to do?" asked Zeke.

"We've got to come up with a plan to stop your family from leaving," said Harris.

"I don't know if that will work," Zeke said sadly.

"C'mon, what do you have to lose?" Harris asked. "We have to at least try!"

"Yes, you're right," said Zeke, starting to feel a little hopeful. "Okay, a plan. So, what's the plan?"

Harris's face scrunched up like it always did when he was deep in thought. "Uh . . . I'm working on it!" Harris paced around the room for a few minutes, and then he suddenly stopped. "Wait, I think I have an idea!"

"WHAT IF THERE WAS A BIG STORM coming?" Harris suggested. "Planes have to wait for storms to clear all the time. It must be the same for spaceships! That might delay them a bit and give us time to come up with a better plan."

"Just a regular storm on Earth wouldn't really stop them," Zeke explained. Then he thought about it a bit longer. "But a space storm might be enough to delay the trip!"

"How are we going to find a space storm?" Harris asked.

"With this," Zeke said. He pulled a small device, about the size of a cell phone, from his pocket.

"What's that?" Harris asked.

"My cosmic imager," said Zeke. "Using this device together with mind projection, we can look deep into space. Watch this."

Zeke pressed the cosmic imager against his forehead. Then he used his mind projection powers to create a huge image of space all around them. Stars suddenly filled up Harris's room.

"Wow!" Harris said. "It's like we're on a ship zooming through outer space."

Huge galaxies spun past them as Zeke pushed his mind projection deeper and deeper into space. A swirling mass of green clouds streaked with orange lightning rushed toward them.

"That's it!" Zeke cried. "It's a huge space storm. And it's in between Earth and Tragas! My parents' spaceship would have to pass right through it in order to get home. This is just what we need. This storm looks so big and dangerous, it could tear the ship in half. My parents would never want to fly through it. Do you know what this means?"

"That we get to hang out together for the whole Spring Break!" Harris said. "And it means that you're not going back to Tragas!"

"I have to go show this to my parents," said Zeke.

Zeke dashed down the stairs and hurried home. He burst through the front door to his house.

"I'm glad to see you've come home," said Xad. "You still have a lot of packing to do, Zeke."

"We can't go," said Zeke.

"Now, we already talked about this, Zeke," said Xad. "Our research is finished and it is time to—"

"No, I mean we *really* can't go," said Zeke. "Look!"

Zeke placed his cosmic imager against his forehead. A star field spread out around him and his parents. In the middle of all the stars, the gaseous space storm raged.

"You see?" said Zeke. "That storm is in our way. We'd have to pass through it to get from Earth back to Tragas."

Quar looked worried. "Zeke is right," she said. "This might delay our return to Tragas for quite a while."

Zeke tried his best not to smile. His plan had worked!

Xad shook his head. "That will not be a problem for us, Zeke," Xad explained. "Before we left Tragas, I installed a new shield for our ship. It is designed to withstand even the strongest storms, as well as solar flares, meteor showers, asteroid fields . . . whatever space throws our way."

"Oh, great," Zeke said with fake enthusiasm.

"Yes, so you see, nothing will stop us from returning to Tragas," said Xad, smiling. "We will all be going home soon."

5 THE DIVERSION

FEELING DEFEATED, ZEKE WALKED slowly back over to Harris's house.

"Our plan didn't work," he said to Harris. "Even a powerful space storm, like the one we saw on the cosmic imager, won't stop my parents from taking me back to Tragas."

"Why not?" asked Harris. "I thought you said that storm could tear your ship in half?"

"My father installed a special shield onto the ship before we left Tragas," Zeke explained. "It can deflect anything it runs into out in space."

"Drats!" Harris flopped onto his bed and stared at the ceiling, trying to think of another way to stop Zeke from leaving. Zeke paced back and forth across the bedroom.

A few seconds later, Harris sat up and jumped off his bed. Zeke could tell that he had a new idea.

"So your parents plan to go home in a spaceship?" Harris asked.

"Yes, the same one we used to travel from Tragas to Earth," Zeke said.

"And where is this ship?" Harris asked.

"In our backyard."

Harris was confused.

"How have you been able to hide it all this time?" he asked. "It must be pretty tiny. I've been in your backyard lots of times. I think I would have noticed a spaceship."

"No, it's actually pretty big," Zeke said. "I can show you, but we can't do it now. My parents are still home packing."

"Hmm . . . what if I ask my parents to invite your parents out to say goodbye?" Harris suggested. "That would give us a chance to check out the spaceship."

"Great idea!" said Zeke, feeling slightly hopeful again.

When Zeke had gone home, Harris spoke with his parents.

"So, Zeke told me that he and his parents are moving back home to Tragas soon," Harris said.

"Oh, I'm sorry to hear that," said his mom. "I've enjoyed getting to know them. They've been great neighbors. And I know that you and Zeke have become such good friends."

"Maybe you can invite them out one last time to say goodbye," Harris suggested.

"A going-away party? That's a great idea," said Harris's mom.

"Why don't we ask them to go bowling?" his dad asked. "That's always fun."

"I like that, yes," said his mom.

Harris's dad called Zeke's parents. Although Xad and Quar had no idea what bowling was, they agreed to go the next night.

"Even though we're done with our research, it is, after all, one last chance to learn about another Earth activity," Xad said to Quar after he hung up the phone.

The next night, once their parents had gone out, Harris headed over to Zeke's house.

"What's bowling?" Zeke asked.

"You take a heavy ball and roll it toward a bunch of wooden pins, trying to knock them over," Harris explained.

"Oh," Zeke said. "That sounds like Breetnot Rolling on Tragas. There, we roll the giant, round fruit of the Breetnot tree toward a group of Bantay sticks, trying to knock them over. But Bantay sticks can move out of the way, so it's really hard."

"Man, games on Tragas sound so cool! I hope I get to see this or Bonkas some day," Harris said as he walked toward the back door. "Okay," he said, "Where's this ship of yours?"

"Come on," said Zeke. "I'll show it to you."

6 THE SHIP

HARRIS AND ZEKE SLIPPED OUT the back door and into the backyard. The entire yard was surrounded by trees so no neighbors could see in.

Harris looked all around.

"Um, I don't see a spaceship, Zeke," he said.

"There it is," Zeke said, pointing at a small metal shed sitting in the far corner of the yard.

"What?" Harris asked. "You keep a super high-tech, galaxy-spanning spaceship that brought you here from Tragas in that rusty, old, piece-of-junk shed?"

"Um, not exactly," Zeke replied. "Actually, that rusty, old, piece-of-junk shed *is* the spaceship."

Harris stared at Zeke, confused. Then he laughed. "And here I thought aliens had better technology!"

"Watch," said Zeke. He pulled the cosmic imager out of his pocket and changed a few settings. Then he pressed a button on the device.

Harris's jaw dropped open in amazement. The rusty, old shed started rumbling and glowing bright green. Harris heard metal creaking and watched as the walls of the shed dropped open, spun around, and started to re-form. The green light grew so bright that Harris had to shield his eyes from it.

When the light faded, a tall and gleaming silver spaceship sat in the spot where the shed had been.

"*That* is our ship," Zeke said. "The shed was a disguise."

"Wow!" said Harris, amazed. "Can we go inside?" he asked eagerly.

Zeke looked around nervously. "Um . . . our parents should be gone for a while, so, come on!"

Zeke pressed another button on his cosmic imager. A door on the side of the ship slid open, and a ladder came down. The two boys climbed up and slipped inside.

Harris was amazed by what he saw. He had read hundreds of comic books and seen many movies about aliens and spaceships, but now here he was, standing inside a *real* one.

Panels of lights flashed and blinked. Screens showed twinkling star fields. And small, flying robots shaped like metal balls zoomed all around, stopping to check and adjust the various controls.

"What are they?" Harris asked, ducking as one of the robots flew past his head.

"Bot-drones," Zeke explained. "All Tragas spaceships use them. They keep all the ship's systems in good-working order."

"Do you know how to fly this thing?" Harris asked, still amazed that he was actually inside his alien friend's spaceship.

"Kind of," Zeke said. "Sometimes, my parents let me operate the controls once we are in deep space, away from any planets, but if you're thinking about taking the ship for a test drive, no, I can't really fly it."

"This is the coolest thing I've ever seen!" Harris said, watching the glowing panels and flying bot-drones.

"Okay, we're here. So what now?" Zeke asked.

Harris looked around. "What if we remove a part of the ship that would stop it from flying?" he suggested.

"That's a good idea," Zeke said. He called up a parts inventory on a viewscreen and scanned through the list.

"I got it!" he said, pointing at the screen.

Zeke bent down and pulled open a panel. Reaching in, he yanked out a small square cube with blinking red lights on all sides.

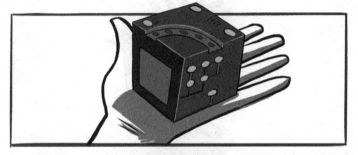

"This is a retro-boost configurator," Zeke said. "It's small, but without it, the ship can't fly. And it would probably take a long time to get a new one delivered from Tragas. This could buy us time to come up with another plan."

Zeke handed the cube to Harris. "I think we should hide this at your house."

Harris nodded. "That makes sense," he said, slipping the cube into his jacket pocket.

The boys hurried out of the ship. Zeke pressed a button on his cosmic imager and the ship transformed back into a rusty, old shed.

"Come on," Zeke said nervously as the two friends headed back over to Harris's house.

BEST-LAID PLANS

ZEKE WOKE UP THE NEXT DAY feeling nervous. It wouldn't take long for his parents to discover that the retro-boost configurator was missing.

What if they figure out that I took it? he wondered. *Maybe I didn't think this plan through as well as I should have.*

After breakfast, Zeke helped his parents load up the spaceship. He slipped boxes, furniture, and various electronic devices into storage compartments. Bot-drones zoomed all around the ship, making sure it was ready for its journey to Tragas.

"Are you feeling any better about going back to Tragas, Zekelabraxis?" Xad asked as he scanned the ship's console with a hand-held analyzer.

"I think so," Zeke said, not really meaning it, but hoping that his plan would keep them on Earth a little longer.

"I am happy to hear that, Zeke," said Xad.

A red light started flashing on Xad's analyzer.

"Hmm . . . one of the bot-drones just uploaded a report," he said. "It appears the retro-boost configurator is missing."

Quar looked concerned. "Well, we can't fly the ship without it," she said.

"It will take weeks for someone from Tragas to get to Earth to deliver a replacement part, right, Xad?" Zeke asked, trying his best to hide his happiness at this delay. "And it's not like there's any place on Earth where you could get one."

"Actually, Zeke, there is a place on Earth," said Xad.

Xad walked off the ship and headed across the backyard. Curious and a bit worried, Zeke followed.

Xad went into the garage, where he had set up a workshop when they first arrived on Earth. Most of it had already been loaded onto the ship, but Xad still had a few shelves full of stuff he hadn't packed yet.

A few minutes later, Xad came back out carrying a brand-new retro-boost configurator. Zeke was shocked, but he didn't say a word.

"Before we left Tragas, I packed spares of a few of the most essential parts of the ship," Xad explained. "I'm not sure what could have happened to the original retro-boost configurator, but it doesn't matter. We've got another one right here."

As Xad and Zeke headed back to the ship, Zeke did his best to hide his disappointment. Back on board, Xad handed the replacement retro-boost configurator to one of the bot-drones, who quickly installed it. The ship's engines hummed to life.

"Let's continue the preflight inspection," said Xad.

Zeke's spirits sank. It appeared now that there was nothing more he could do. He was leaving Earth for good, and going back to Tragas.

8 THE LAST DAY

THE NEXT DAY, ZEKE WENT OVER to Harris's house. He was not looking forward to telling his friend that their plan had failed. It really looked like nothing would delay his return to Tragas. And worse, he had to break the news to Harris that he was leaving that night.

"It didn't work," Zeke said sadly. "My dad had an extra part. So this is the last day we have to spend together."

Harris shook his head. He didn't want to accept the fact that he would never see his friend again.

"Maybe there is another way to sabotage the ship," Harris said. "Maybe we could—"

But Zeke cut him off.

"It's no use, Harris," he said. "We tried. I'm leaving tonight and there's nothing we can do to change that. So let's just enjoy our last day together as much as we can, okay?"

Harris nodded. "Okay," he said. "What do you want to do?"

"Let's throw the ball around," said Zeke. "Of all the things I've learned about Earth, baseball is one of the most fun."

The boys got their baseball gloves and started tossing a ball back and forth.

"Remember when you thought you had to use your powers to help you play baseball?" Harris asked as he threw a high pop-up toward Zeke.

"Yes," said Zeke, settling under the ball and catching it in his glove. "But it's much more fun to just play the game correctly."

"What next?" Harris asked after they had played catch for a while.

"I think I'm really going to miss chocolate," Zeke said.

Harris smiled. "I have one box left over from Valentine's Day. Come on."

Zeke and Harris ran into the house. Harris pulled out a box of chocolates and the boys ate every last one.

"What now?" Harris asked, wiping his mouth with the back of his sleeve.

"What would *you* like to do, Harris?" Zeke asked, following Harris's lead and smearing chocolate all over his sleeve.

"*Monster Mania!*" Harris said.

Monster Mania was a virtual reality video game that Zeke had brought from Tragas.

"Great!" said Zeke. He ran over to his house and returned with two helmets. The boys placed the helmets onto their heads.

For the next hour, they were lost in a virtual world. They battled fire-breathing dragons, fierce dinosaurs, and an army of angry trolls.

But before they knew it, the day had slipped by and it was time for Zeke to leave.

"Well, this is it, Zeke," said Harris.

"Don't be sad, Harris," said Zeke, though he was feeling very sad himself. "I promise to stay in touch with trans-galactic vmail messages."

Harris nodded.

"And who knows, maybe I'll get back to Earth some day," Zeke said.

Harris laughed and hugged Zeke.

"Or maybe I'll get to Tragas some day," Harris said. "We'll always be friends, no matter what."

Zeke smiled, and then he walked out the front door.

Harris sat alone in his room, feeling as lonely as he'd ever felt.

I CAN'T STAND JUST SITTING HERE feeling lonely and sad, Harris thought. He decided to call Roxy to see if she could come over.

A short while later, she arrived.

"Why so sad?" Roxy asked, seeing Harris's expression.

"It's Zeke," Harris said.

"Zeke? Is he alright?" Roxy asked, sounding worried.

"No . . . I mean, yes. He's okay, but no." Harris stumbled over his words, getting more and more upset.

"Okay, calm down and just tell me what's going on," Roxy said.

"Zeke's going home," Harris said.

"Home? You mean to Tragas?" Roxy asked.

Harris nodded. "His parents' research here is done."

"Oh, wow. That is sad," Roxy said. "But, hey, we can go visit him in Tragas. I think it would be fun to visit another country." She was doing her best to try to cheer him up.

Harris looked away. He thought about how when Zeke arrived, he tried to prove that Zeke was an alien. Then he thought about how Zeke trusted him and told him the truth, and how he did everything he could since then to protect his friend's secret.

He always felt bad about lying to Roxy. She was Zeke's friend, too, and she was Harris's best friend. They never had a secret between them, except for this one.

Well, that's about to change, Harris thought. He was sure that Zeke wouldn't be upset about him telling Roxy. *Zeke trusted me, and I trust Roxy.*

"Roxy," Harris said. "Tragas is not a country . . . it's a planet."

"A *planet*?" Roxy asked, confused. "What are you talking about? Wait . . . you're not going to start with that 'Zeke is an alien stuff' again just because he's leaving, are you?!" Roxy asked, shaking her head. "I thought you were over that. You're his friend now!"

"Did you ever notice all the cool gadgets and high-tech gear Zeke has?" Harris asked. "Like this!" Harris pulled the retro-boost configurator out of his pocket and showed it to Roxy. "It all comes from the planet Tragas."

"That doesn't prove anything," said Roxy hesitantly.

"Remember in school that time when that bag of flour almost hit Zeke on the head?" Harris asked. "But at the last second, the bag moved all by itself and landed on Mr. Mulvaney instead? And his costume? That's what he actually looks like."

"Yeah, but—"

"And how fast Zeke was able to get really good at baseball when he had never even played before?"

"Well, that still doesn't prove any—"

"And how he thought that giving someone a bucket of worms was a way of saying 'I like you'?"

"Okay, that was really strange. But I still don't think it's true," Roxy said.

Harris noticed something on the floor near his desk. He walked over and picked up Zeke's cosmic imager.

This must have fallen out of Zeke's pocket!

"It's true, Roxy," Harris said. "And I can prove it!"

10 ALL ABOARD

HARRIS LED ROXY OVER TO ZEKE'S backyard. He pointed the cosmic imager at the old shed and pressed the button he had seen Zeke press. Once again, the shed went through its shifting, glowing transformation, changing into a spaceship.

Watching wide-eyed, Roxy was stunned. She finally realized that Harris had been telling the truth about Zeke all along.

"Why didn't you *tell* me?" Roxy asked.

Harris rolled his eyes. "I tried!" he said. "I tried to tell everyone, remember? But no one believed me. Zeke only told me himself after I got in trouble for trying to prove it, but he asked me to keep it a secret."

Roxy nodded. "I appreciate what a good friend you've been to him, protecting him and keeping his secret from everyone."

"Come on," said Harris. "I'll show you something really cool!"

Harris led Roxy onto the spaceship.

"This is amazing!" she said, looking at all the high-tech equipment and watching the bot-drones buzz through the air. "I've never seen anything like it. I can't believe . . . Zeke and his parents are aliens!"

Suddenly, they heard footsteps entering the ship.

"Oh, no!" whispered Harris. "We'll get caught! Quick, hide!"

Harris and Roxy opened a storage cabinet and slipped inside, pulling the door closed behind them. From their hiding place, they heard voices.

"Zeke, did you forget to change the ship back into its shed disguise when we finished loading?" Quar asked.

"I don't think so," Zeke said, confused. "But I might have hit the button on my cosmic imager by accident."

Zeke reached into his pocket to check the device. *It's not here!* he thought. *Where did I leave it?*

"Well, no matter," said Xad. "It is time to go home. Bot-drones, prepare the ship for takeoff."

Crouched in their hiding place, Harris and Roxy felt the ship's engines rumble to life.

"We're trapped!" Harris whispered.

"How are we going to get off this ship?" Roxy asked. "My parents told me to be home for dinner!"

Before Harris could reply, the door to the cabinet swung open. Looking out, Harris and Roxy saw Zeke staring back at them in shock.

A big smile spread across Zeke's face.

The three friends heard the engines get louder, then they felt the ship leave the ground, gaining speed as it streaked toward space.

Harris looked at Zeke, then at Roxy. "Well, guys," he said. "I guess we're *all* going to Tragas!"

READ ON FOR A SNEAK PEAK
FROM THE FIRST BOOK IN THE
ISLE OF MISFITS SERIES!

———— CHAPTER ONE ————

THE LONELIEST GARGOYLE

Gibbon the gargoyle lived atop the same castle all his life. Gargoyles were meant to protect the buildings they lived on. Sometimes, that meant protecting the people inside those buildings, too. That's what Gibbon was always taught.

But Gibbon couldn't stay still in one place *all* day. Sure, it was what he was *supposed* to do, but it was boring! So Gibbon found something new to do to pass the time: playing pranks on people as they walked by below.

And winter was his favorite season for pranks. Winter meant snowballs.

One snowy day, he saw a man in a suit hurrying by the castle. Gibbon quickly made a snowball in his hands. He held it over the edge and dropped it, watching as it hit the man right on the head.

The man jumped from the shock of the cold snow. A confused look crossed his face when he didn't see anyone around. Holding back laughter, Gibbon rolled another snowball and dropped it on the man. This time, the man yelped and ran off.

"*Gibbon!*" a voice whispered harshly.

He jumped and turned toward the gargoyle speaking to him. Elroy was the leader of the castle gargoyles and almost never broke his silence.

"That's enough," Elroy ordered. "You are too old to be playing pranks on the humans. You need to start taking your post seriously."

"But it's so boring!" Gibbon protested. "We just stand around all day. Even at night, we do nothing! What are we even defending the castle from anyway?"

Elroy did not move, but his eyes glared over at Gibbon. "You need to learn how to work with your team, Gibbon. Your slacking off only makes it harder for the rest of us."

With a sigh, Gibbon looked down at the street. He watched as a group of kids stopped below the castle. One of them picked up some snow and threw it at another. Instead of getting mad, the other kid started laughing and made his own snowball. In no time at all, the kids were in a full-fledged snowball fight!

That's what I want, Gibbon thought. For a very long time, Gibbon watched people's lives from the top of the castle. A lot of them had friends and family and fun, but Gibbon didn't really have any of that. The other gargoyles never wanted to play or laugh. They only wanted to watch the world as it went by.

Maybe if I can get Elroy to play, everyone else will loosen up! he thought.

Gibbon smiled. "Hey, Elroy. Catch me if you can! If you do, I'll sit still and guard the castle the rest of the day!"

With a laugh, Gibbon took off. He climbed down the side of the castle, then darted down an empty street.

Gibbon knew—he just *knew*—if Elroy played with him, he'd understand.

But when he stopped and looked back, he didn't see Elroy. His heart sank.

A. I. NEWTON always wanted to travel into space, visit another planet, and meet an alien. When that didn't work out, he decided to do the next best thing—write stories about aliens! The Alien Next Door series gives him a chance to imagine what it's like to hang out with an alien. And you can do the same—unless you're lucky enough to live next door to a real-life alien!

ANJAN SARKAR graduated from Manchester Metropolitan University with a degree in illustration. He worked as an illustrator and graphic designer before becoming a freelancer, where he now gets to work on all sorts of different illustration projects! He lives in Sheffield, England.

anjansarkar.co.uk

**LOOK FOR MORE BOOKS IN
THE *ALIEN NEXT DOOR* SERIES!**

Journey to some magical places, rock out, and find your inner superhero with these other chapter book series from **Little Bee Books!**

little bee books
an imprint of Bonnier Publishing USA